Up, Up the Mountain

Up, Up the Mountain

by AILEEN FISHER

Illustrated by GILBERT RISWOLD

Thomas Y. Crowell Company, New York

By the Author

BEST LITTLE HOUSE

GOING BAREFOOT

I LIKE WEATHER

IN THE MIDDLE OF THE NIGHT

LIKE NOTHING AT ALL

LISTEN, RABBIT

MY MOTHER AND I

UP, UP THE MOUNTAIN

WHERE DOES EVERYONE GO?

Manufactured in the United States of America
L.C. Card 68-11060

1   2   3   4   5   6   7   8   9   10

To E. R.,
remembering Blue Lake
and the trail to Niwot

One year we had summer
instead of winter.

One year we had summer
when spring was here.

It wasn't the fault
of the calendar printer
that we had *summer*
for all the year . . .

It was because
we had gone away
far to the south
for a long, long stay,
where palm trees clattered
and sea gulls chattered
and breakers spattered
a rim of spray
over the beach
and backed away,
and weather was summery
every day.

No frost on hedges,
no hills for skis,
no snow-white edges
on twigs of trees,

No tingly shivers,
no snowball fights,
no ice on rivers,
no snowed-in nights,

No sudden peeping
of crocus heads
out of the sleeping
garden beds.

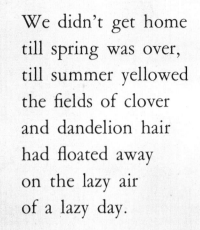

We didn't get home
till spring was over,
till summer yellowed
the fields of clover
and dandelion hair
had floated away
on the lazy air
of a lazy day.

"Summer," I said,
"is sunny and nice,
but we had it once
and we had it *twice,*
and nobody wants it
again so soon . . .
I'd rather have May,
I'd rather have June,
or April with frost
and a cold white moon."

"And I!" said Mother.
"I miss the sight
of springtime springing up
overnight."

"And wind," said my brother,
"for flying a kite."

Then Father blinked
in a thoughtful way,
and I was amazed
to hear him say,
"Rather have April?
Rather have May?
It's really not
an impossible thing.
Let's drive through summer
and walk to spring!"

He chuckled. "And maybe
before we're through
we could see something
of winter, too."

I hadn't an inkling
of what he meant,
for how could we see
a spring event
like leaves uncrinkling,
and bluebells tinkling,
and snowflakes twinkling
when spring was *spent*?

But we packed the car
and away we went!

My brother whispered:
"I bet *I* know.
We'll drive up north
where there still is snow,
as far to the north
as a car can go."

But my brother's ideas
aren't always best.
We didn't go north.
We headed *west*.

We crossed a river
the color of zinc,

We drove where fences
ran by in a wink,

We faced a sunset
more orange than pink,

We crossed a prairie
that needed a drink . . .

And *still* I didn't
know what to think.

Drive through summer
and walk to spring?
It seemed the most
impossible thing.

Then blue and humpy,
humpy and high,
at the end of the prairie
dusty-dry,
we saw some mountains
that rimmed the sky.

Mother cried, "Look!"

And Father said, "Soon
I'll show you colors
like May and June . . .
buttercup yellow
and springtime green
and larkspur purple
and air washed clean."

Oh, but it's fun
to be almost there
when you don't know *where*.

Oh, but it's fun
to be looking a lot
for you-don't-know-what.

We reached a place
that was steep and narrow
where a stream hopped down
as quick as a sparrow.

We reached a place
where the car went slower
and Tops looked higher
and Bottoms lower.

We bumped along
till Father said, "Whoa!
This is as far
as a car can go,
with mountains around,
above, below.

"We'll camp all night,
and I give you warning
you'd better sleep tight
for in the morning
we'll start up a trail
with a peak to scale.

"For here's where
a mountain trail begins,
before the green
of the forest thins
and faces of crags
lift up their chins."

Instead of being pent
in the dark old tent
my brother and I
lay under the sky
in sleeping bags
as the night went by.

Spruces were spires
of a woodsy church,
and some of the stars
came down to perch,
and a sickle of moon
cut through the dark,
and a meteor fell
like a blown-out spark,
and we heard an owl . . .
then a coyote bark.

And in the morning,
the funniest thing—
summer was gone
and the air smelled *spring,*
washed and dampish,
and fresh and clean,
and the grass by the stream
was frosty green.

And Mother said, "Oh,
it's the strangest thing
in the middle of summer
to wake to spring!
The sun is caught
in the roof of trees.
Who would have thought
We'd almost freeze?"

We shivered and shook
and quivered and quook,
and quivered and quaked
and shivered and shaked,
till the fire blazed up
and all of us stood
warming ourselves
and feeling good,

Smelling the firs
and spicy spruces,
and frosty dampness
that night unlooses,
and bacon sizzling
in sizzly juices,
and coffee boiling,
and campfire smoke . . .

A stick fell out
and they let me poke!

"It's a possible thing
to catch up with spring
without much bother
at all," said Father.

"*Every* one thousand feet
 we climb
 up a mountain
 most any time,
 up through the woods
 and past the trees,
 weather gets colder
 by three degrees—
 about the same
 as driving as far
 as six hundred miles
 to the north by car!

"That's how weathery
 mountains are."

"Think!" said Mother,
 whose smile was gay,
"the gallons of gas
 we'll save today
 when we climb the trail
 where the conies stay,
 those quick little creatures
 in buff and gray."

"Let's," said Father,
"be on our way."

The trail went zigging,
the trail went zagging
up through the woods
where the sun was lagging,
up toward the peaks
that pierced the sky,
up where the blue
shone bright and high,
up, up the mountain.

"Larkspur!" cried Mother
  with happy squeaks.
"At home it's been gone
  for weeks and weeks.

"And see the buttercups,
harebells, too,
and violets, white
as well as blue,
still full of blossoms,
looking new."

"Grass and clover
  as fresh as day,"
said Father. "There isn't
  a sign of hay."

"And tips on the trees!"
  my brother said,
"Look at the spring-green
  tips ahead."

Up, up . . .
sky is a cup
of shiny blue
and bottom-side-up,
washed and new,
new and bright,
sky is a cup
of sparkly light
up, up the mountain.

The higher we climbed,
the shorter the trees,
until they were crawling
on hands and knees,
until they were actually
lying right down
in windrows of green
and tangles of brown.

"Wind," said Father,
"snips with its snippers,
nips with its nippers,
clips with its clippers.
Wind," said Father,
"prunes and trims
twigs and boughs
and leaves and limbs.

"Some of these trees
are older by far
than all of our ages
together are,
but they haven't a chance
to grow up tall,
with cold and blizzards
and wind and all."

Over some rocks
a cony streaked,
and one of his cousins
eeked and squeaked.

We found a wonderful
bank of snow
(not as white
as in winter, though),
crouching beneath
some rocks; and so
we all had snowballs,
at last, to throw!

At the edge of the snow
some buds were breaking
and clumps of grass
were only just waking,
as if it were April,
as if it were May,
and not a calendar's
summer day.

"To me," said Mother,
"the sun seems warm
here in the open.
No sign of storm . . .
let's hide our sweaters
beside the trail,
behind the boulders
and piles of shale."

But Father said, "No.
Although it's true
the sky looks perfectly
clear and blue,
you never can tell
what weather will do
on a mountainside
in an hour or two.

"Tie your sweaters
around your waist
in case you need them
again . . . in haste."

Up, up
where the high peaks show
with streaks and patches
of melting snow.

Up, up
where the air is thin
and sunburn pinkens
your nose and skin.
Up, up the mountain.

Oh, but it's fun
to be really *there,*
when you didn't know where!

Oh, but it's fun
to be up as high
as the wings of the sky!

We saw some pinks
in a cushion of moss
with heads too low
for the wind to toss.

We saw some dwarf
little bells and phlox
hugging the warmth
between the rocks,
snug as a garden
inside a box.

Then we ate our lunch,
and looked through the glasses
at heights and canyons
and peaks and passes,
and lay on the tundra
(that's what the grass is).

Then after a while
the sun went under.

The sky lost its smile.

A roll of thunder
echoed across
a mountain gap,
and the wind came up
with a snap and a slap,
and I wished I'd taken
a coonskin cap.

On with the sweaters!
Button them tight!
Rain hid the mountain peaks
from sight.

We huddled together
behind the stones
with quivers and shivers
in all our bones.

Lightning flashed
and thunder rumbled
and crag after crag
on the mountains grumbled,
and clouds dipped low
and some of them stumbled . . .
and out of their pockets
snowflakes tumbled.

"I s-s-said," cried Father,
    whose lips were blue,
"we might see something
    of winter, t-t-too,
    before we were th-through."

It didn't last long.
We didn't quite freeze . . .
though we shook in our teeth
and shook in our knees
up on the mountain
above the trees
in the wintry breeze.

Then a brand new
shined-up sun peeked out
through a hole in the sky
like a weather scout,
and shimmery snowflakes
round about
flashed and twinkled
and flickered out.

We ran down the trail
with a whoop and a shout,

Quick as a cony,
light as a feather,
glad we had found
the promised weather,
all of the seasons
mixed together,

Yet glad to go
down the slope to borrow
a bit of summer
until tomorrow . . .

when another trail
with a peak to scale
would lead through the woods
and across the shale
up, up the mountain.